LITTI

PRAYER

LITTLE BOOK *on* PRAYER

REV JUSTIN GRIFFIN

TATE PUBLISHING
AND ENTERPRISES, LLC

Little Book on Prayer

Published by Tate Publishing & Enterprises, LLC
127 E. Trade Center Terrace | Mustang, Oklahoma 73064 USA
1.888.361.9473 | www.tatepublishing.com

Tate Publishing is committed to excellence in the publishing industry. The company reflects the philosophy established by the founders, based on Psalm 68:11,
"The Lord gave the word and great was the company of those who published it."

Cover design by Allen Jomoc
Interior design by Caypeeline Casas

Published in the United States of America

ISBN: 978-1-63306-579-6
Religion / Christian Life / Prayer
14.08.15

PREFACE

This study primarily uses R. A. Torrey's book *How to Pray* as a chapter-by-chapter walk-through. It also draws from E. M. Bounds's *Power through Prayer* and James Orr's *How to Live a Holy Life*.

Furthermore, this study also extrapolated a few thoughts from Brother Lawrence's *The Practice of the Presence of God*, Andrew Murray's *Absolute Surrender* and a word or two from C. H. Spurgeon's *Morning and Evening Readings*.

Importantly, all the above materials were found in the public domain, and they have been rephrased, summarized, adapted, and focused according to the comprehension of Pastor Griffin into this little book on prayer.

Unless otherwise indicated, all scriptures used in this book are taken from the King James Version. These scriptures are taken from the 1769 Cambridge edition of the King James Version of the Bible.

This book is dedicated to the LORD God Almighty (YHWH). On the front cover is the personal name of our God written in Hebrew, which in English translates as *YHWH*. Following the custom of the King James translators, every time the personal name of God is used throughout this study, the word LORD is used instead of *YHWH*. To see why Jehovah is not God's name, see appendix B.

INTRODUCTION

If one desires to have a deeper relationship with the only living God of the universe, then this little book on prayer can help. Yet, one needs to read this book through the Holy Spirit that dwells within oneself. Simply being smart or sophisticated will not help someone understand the teachings in this book. Intelligence and education are good, but true believers are to look to God the Holy Spirit to lead them, especially when it concerns spiritual matters such as those discussed in this work.

Also, while reading this book, one should stay in constant communication with the Almighty. Pray, meditate, and talk to God the Father, God the Son, and God the Holy Spirit as you use this little book on prayer. Furthermore, this book was not written to make one feel bad or guilty about one's prayer life. No, this book was written to bring to light the spiritual power available to those who are indwelt with God the Holy Spirit (Romans 5:5, Corinthians 6:19, KJV).

Finally, this book covers a very important issue. To cavalierly handle this book by only skimming and not fully reading it will do more to impair the reader than prepare the reader to fully comprehend how the Holy Spirit, the Bible, the believer, and prayer all work together.

The author strongly recommends you thoroughly read this book twice with a pen in hand. Read the book completely the first time to ensure that you fully grasp the main idea, and then read the study a second time to grasp the finer points. As you read, mark areas of interest. Underline those sentences or paragraphs that you want to explore further. Circle the page number of a particular page that you may want to return to later. Write your thoughts and feelings in the margins as you read. Finally, take time to give a prayerful answer to all the questions.[1]

LIFT UP YOUR PRAYERS TO THE LORD

What do you want to thank or praise God for?

What do you want to ask of your LORD?

Whose life would you like God to touch?

What situation are you facing right now for which you want God's intervention?

1

1. In the sixth chapter of Ephesians in the eighteenth verse, we read inspirational words that proclaim the tremendous importance of prayer with startling and overwhelming force. The Ephesians passage reads:

> Praying always with all prayer and supplication in the Spirit, and watching thereunto with all perseverance and supplication for all saints.
>
> (KJV)

1.1 Praying always: The message communicated in this part of the verse is consistent communication and meditation with the Almighty throughout one's life. According to this verse, we should seek to establish ourselves in God's Presence by continually conversing with Him. Yet, know this: there is a vast difference between praying *at* God and communicating *with* God.

Q1. When was the last time we Christians had a consistent conversation with God, in which we were talking with Him and not just at Him?

1.2 In the Spirit: If then we would pray aright, the first thing that we should do is know that we are really in the presence of the LORD. Before a word of request is made, we should have a definite and vivid consciousness that we are talking to God Almighty and know that He is listening. However, since this is only possible by the Holy Spirit's power, we should look to the Holy Spirit to lead us into the presence of God. Yet how shall we attain this earnestness in prayer? Not by trying to work ourselves up into it. The true method is explained in Romans 8:5, which says, "For they that are after the flesh do mind the things of the flesh; but they that are after the Spirit the things of the Spirit" (KJV). The earnestness that we work up in the energy of the flesh is a repulsive thing.

On the other hand, the earnestness forged in us by the power of the Holy Spirit is pleasing to God. Here again, if we would pray aright to enter into the presence of God, to have a definite vivid consciousness of God, we must look to God the Holy Spirit to teach us to pray. For thus says

God's Word, "But the Comforter, *which is* the Holy Ghost, whom the Father will send in my name, he shall teach you all things" (John 14:26, KJV).

Q2. When is the last time one prayed something like this: "Holy Spirit, please teach me how to pray?" or "Please lead me into the presence of God," then stopped and listened and waited for the Holy Spirit to respond?

1.3 Continuing with Ephesians 6:18, we read the words "Watching thereunto," more literally, "being sleepless thereunto." Apostle Paul realized the natural slothfulness of people and especially their natural slothfulness toward prayer.

Q3. Is it possible that our modern prayer has no power in it because there is no heart in it? What? We rush into God's presence, throw a string of requests at the LORD, jump up, and go out. If we put so little heart into our prayers, then why do we expect God to put much heart into answering them?

2. One of the most significant verses in the Bible on prayer is first John 3:22. John says, "And whatsoever we ask, we receive of him, because we keep his commandments, and do those things that are pleasing in his sight."

   2.1 "Whatsoever I ask I receive?" Yes! John explains why this was so: "because we keep His commandments, and do those things that are pleasing in His sight." In other words, the one who expects God to do as he or she asks Him must on their part do whatever the LORD bids them and do it out of their unconditional love for their Creator.

   2.2 If we give a listening ear to all God's commands to us, He will give a listening ear to all our appeals to Him. If, on the other hand, we turn a deaf ear to the precepts of the LORD of Hosts, He will be likely to turn a deaf ear to our prayers. Here we find the secret of much unanswered prayer. We are not listening to God's Word, and therefore, He is not listening to our prayers. What? Is that possible?

      Q4. Does the Bible really teach that God will not listen to every prayer? Consider the answer from God's Word:

- But your iniquities have separated between you and your God, and your sins have hid *his* face from you, that he will not hear" (Isaiah 59:2, KJV).
- Now we know that God heareth not sinners: but if any man be a worshipper of God, and doeth his will, him he heareth" (John 9:31, KJV).
- "If I regard iniquity in my heart, the LORD will not hear *me*" (Psalms 66:18, KJV).
- "Then shall they call upon me, but I will not answer; they shall seek me early, but they shall not find me: For that they hated knowledge, and did not choose the fear of the LORD" (Proverbs 1:28–29, KJV).

As far as man-made theories go, most Christians have heard that "God is always listening and He always answers all prayers." The problem with this theory is that it does not take into consideration passages of Scripture like the above.

Following all the teachings on God and prayer, it is true that God may listen and answer "yes" or "no" or "wait" to a prayer, but it is just as equally true that God does not even have to hear the prayer offered by the unrepentant and willfully disobedient sinner.

We Christians know that the Bible does not contradict itself, and yes, the Bible has lots of verses that say that God will listen. However, the Bible also has lots of verses that say He does not have to listen. The verses on God listening or not listening do not contradict one another but perfectly harmonize with one another. How?

If God says He will listen or not listen, then He can do that because He is God. God can do whatever He wants the way He wants, and the Almighty is not constrained by man's limited ability to comprehend what He does or doesn't do (Daniel 4:35, KJV).

Furthermore, one can use prayer shawls, prayer beads, prayer rugs, or any physical prayer thingy they think will help their prayers to get to God; but if they are in willful, unrepentant sin, then the Bible is clear that God does not have to hear them.

One needs neither crafty arts nor mechanical contrivances for going to God in prayer, but only a humble repentant heart determined to apply itself to nothing but God and to unconditionally love Him and Him only[1]. For thus saith the Word of the LORD:

> The LORD our God is one LORD: And thou shalt love the LORD thy God with all thy heart, and with all thy soul, and with all thy mind, and with all thy strength… And these words, which I command thee this day, shall be in thine heart…[2]"

We have one God. "For there are three that bear record in heaven, the Father, the Word, and the Holy Ghost: and these three are one"[3]. We are to love our one God with the totality of our being, and thus should we be praying to our one God with the totality of our being.

2

Prayer is the energy and life of a Christian's soul. It is the invincible armor that shields the devoted Christian from the poisoned missiles shot forth from the cannons of hell. It is the mighty weapon with which he fights life's battles unto victory. The one who lives in prayer reigns triumphant. The dark storm clouds are driven away; mountains of discouragement are cast into the sea; chasms of difficulties are bridged; hope is given wings; faith increases; and joys abound. Hell may rage and threaten; but the one who is frequent and fervent in prayer experiences no alarm[1].

1. Psalms 145:18 throws light on the question of how to pray: "The LORD *is* nigh unto all them that call upon him, to all that call upon him in truth" (KJV).

   1.1 The expression *in truth* means *in reality*, or *in sincerity*. Thus, the prayer that the Trinity answers is the prayer that is real, the prayer that asks for something that is sincerely desired.

Q5. Yet aren't all prayers real and sincere? Do we Christians pray for a revival? Are we willing to pray "Holy Spirit come and bring revival no matter the cost and no matter the change?"

1.2 Many a church that may be praying for a revival does not really desire a true Holy Spirit revival. They think they do, for to their minds a revival means an increase of membership, an increase of income, and an increase of reputation among the other churches.

However, if they knew what a real Holy Spirit revival meant, what a searching of souls on the part of professed Christians would take place. What a purging and shaking up of the church would come, and many other *changes* would come to pass if God the Holy Spirit was poured out in reality and power. If all these were known, would the real cry of the church be for revival?

Yes, when God brings His children to the place where we really desire the conversion of friends and family at any cost, really desire the outpouring of God the Holy Spirit whatever it may involve, really desire the baptism with the Holy Spirit come what may, where we desire anything "in truth" and then call upon God for it "in truth," then the Bible teaches that God is open to hear the prayers of His Children.

2. Jesus spoke a wonderful word about prayer to His disciples on the night before His crucifixion. He said, "And whatsoever ye shall ask in my name, that will I do, that the Father may be glorified in the Son. If ye shall ask any thing in my name, I will do *it*" (John 14:13, 14, KJV).

    2.1 Prayer in the name of Christ has power with God. God the Father is well pleased with His only begotten Son, the LORD Jesus Christ. He hears Him always, and He also always hears the prayer that is truly in His name. There is a fragrance in the name of Christ that makes acceptable to God every prayer that bears it.

        Q6. But what is it to pray in the name of the LORD Jesus Christ? Is it merely a verbal period at the end of a prayer or some kind of magical incantation?

    2.2 Concerning praying in the name of the LORD Jesus Christ, many explanations have been made, but many do not explain what it means. But there is nothing magical or mysterious about this expression. If one will go through the Bible and examine all the passages in which the expression "in My name" or "in His name" or synonymous expressions are used, one will find that it means to come in that person's *authority*.

Praying in the name of Christ is not just adding the phrase "I ask these things in Jesus's name" to my prayer. I may put that phrase in my prayer and be resting in my own abilities and merit all the time. But when I do approach God, not on the ground of my merit but on the ground of Christ's merit, not on the ground of my goodness but on the ground of the atoning blood[2], God will hear me. God will hear me, because He is hearing the power of Christ through me.

> Q7. Is it possible that many Christians are ending their prayers with the phrase "in the name of Jesus" and have next-to-no idea what it means to actually pray in the name, that is to pray in the authority or power of the LORD Jesus Christ?

3. Praying in God's Will: "And this is the confidence that we have in him, that, if we ask any thing according to his will, he heareth us: And if we know that he hear us, whatsoever we ask, we know that we have the petition that we desired of him" (1 John 5:14, 15, KJV). This passage plainly teaches us that if we are to pray aright, the

righteous must pray according to God's will, then we will be beyond merely "wishing we get" and will receive the thing we ask of the LORD.

Q8. But can we know the will of God? Can we know that any specific prayer is according to His Holy Divine will?

3.1 We most surely can! How? By God's Word, the Bible. The LORD of Hosts has revealed His will in His Word. Here is one of the greatest secrets of prevailing prayer: to study the Bible to discover God's will as revealed there in His decrees, and then simply take these decrees and spread them out before God in prayer with an unwavering expectation that He will do what He has declared in His Word.

But what are the decrees of the LORD, one may ask? The decrees of the LORD are those statements in the Bible in which it is avowed that God shall do something. Furthermore, since the Bible is inspired by our God of truth, then all the decrees of the LORD will be done as God has arranged to do them. As a final point, the decrees of the LORD are also referred to as promises, since whatever the LORD avowed to do is as a guaranty that it will be done.

3.2 When anything is distinctly promised or decreed in the Word of God, we know that it is His will to give that thing. If then when I pray, I can find some definite decree of the LORD and lay that declaration before the LORD, I know that He hears me, and if I know that the Almighty hears me, I know that I have the petition that I have asked of Him.

Q9. What if one tries to cobble up decrees out of God's Word? Is that person truly praying in God's will, in accordance with what God has declared? Why?

3

> If you desire to be more deeply and sincerely aligned with God's will, pray. If you desire heights in His love, depths in His grace, fullness in His joy, and richness in His glory, pray, meditate, and talk with the Almighty with all sincerity of heart and intensity of soul. Saying you have "no time for prayer" is very dangerous. Regular neglect of spiritual communication with the only living God of the universe must result in a lukewarm Christian.[1]

1. In Ephesians 6:18 and Jude 20, we find a divine guide that leads and teaches a saved soul how to pray. That guide in a few words is "God the Holy Spirit."

> Praying always with all prayer and supplication in the Spirit…But ye, beloved, building up yourselves on your most holy faith, praying in the Holy Ghost (KJV).

1.1 True prayer is prayer in the Spirit; that is, the prayer the Holy Spirit inspires and directs. When we come into the Almighty's presence, we should recognize our infirmity, our ignorance of what we should pray for or how we should pray for it. In the consciousness of our utter inability to pray aright, we should look to the Holy Spirit, utterly casting ourselves upon Him to lead and direct our prayers and to guide our presentation of them.

Praying in the Holy Spirit is praying in fervency. Cold prayers ask the LORD not to hear them. Those who do not plead with fervency do not plead at all. One may as well speak of lukewarm fire as of lukewarm praying.[2] Here are three aids to deeper, fervent prayer:

(1) The foundation of a powerful prayer life is humility, but what is humility? Humility or humbleness is to know our place before God. Humbleness and true fervent praying start when the Holy Spirit opens us to the spiritual realization that God is the Creator and we are His finite creations; that God is our Master and we are His servants; that God is our Father and we are His children; that God is our King and we are His subjects; and that God is our High Priest and we are His priesthood of believers. Again,

true fervent praying starts when we know our place before the blessed Trinity and rejoice therein.

(2) When we first come into God's presence, we should be silent before Him. We should look to the Holy Spirit to teach us how to pray. We must wait for the Holy Spirit and be open to the Spirit. Then we shall pray aright; we shall pray fervently.

(3) Oftentimes when we come to God in prayer, we do not feel like praying. What shall one do in such a case? Not pray until one does feel like it? Not at all. When we least feel like praying is the time when we most need to pray and pray fervently. We should tell Him how cold and prayerless our hearts are and look up to Him and trust Him to warm our hearts and draw them out in fervent prayer.

Q10. Think of humbleness and quietness in praying. Is it possible that some churchgoing people are not willing to be humbled before the LORD or to wait quietly while praying? Is it possible that we have erected golden calves of distraction around our prayer life that keep us from fervent prayer?

2. If we are to pray with power, we must pray with faith. In Mark 11:24, Jesus says, "Therefore I say unto you, What things soever ye desire, when ye pray, believe that ye receive *them*, and ye shall have *them*" (KJV). No matter how clear any decree of God's Word may be, we will not enjoy it in actual experience unless we confidently expect its fulfillment in answer to our prayer.

    2.1 "If any of you lack wisdom," says James, "let him ask of God that giveth to all *men* liberally, and upbraideth not; and it shall be given him" (James 1:5, KJV). Now that declaration is as clear as a decree of the LORD can be, and the next verse adds, "But let him ask in faith, nothing wavering. For he that wavereth is like a wave of the sea driven with the wind and tossed." If one is to pray with the power of the Almighty's decrees, they must pray with faith!

    Yes, there is a faith that goes beyond academic knowledge, that goes beyond emotionalism, and that goes beyond expectation, which believes that the prayer is heard and the decree granted. This comes out in the Mark 11:24, saying, "Therefore I say unto you, What things soever ye desire, when ye pray, believe that ye receive *them*, and ye shall have *them*."

Q11. But how does one receive this kind of faith, this kind of trusting and believing, this kind of faith that is not stifled with doubting and double-mindedness?

2.2 Let us say with all emphasis it cannot be pumped up that is manifested in the flesh, for thus says the Word of God:

> For they that are after the flesh do mind the things of the flesh; but they that are after the Spirit the things of the Spirit. For to be carnally minded *is* death; but to be spiritually minded *is* life and peace. Because the carnal mind *is* enmity against God: for it is not subject to the law of God, neither indeed can be. So then they that are in the flesh cannot please God.
>
> Romans 8:5–8 (KJV)

Many people read the decree in Mark 11:24 about the prayer of faith and then ask for things that they desire and try to *make* themselves believe that God has heard the prayer. This only ends in disappointment, for they are not exercising real Christian faith and the thing is not granted.

It is at this point that many people make a collapse of faith altogether, trying to work up faith by an effort of their will. Since the thing they made themselves believe they expected to get is not given, the very foundation of true faith is undermined by the flesh

> Prayer is the breath, the watchword, the comfort, the strength, and the honour of a Christian. Yet, only the prayer which comes from God can go back to God. Thus, the desire which He writes upon our heart will move His heart and bring down blessings, but the desires of the flesh have no power with God. A prayerless soul is a Christless soul, and the prayers of a fleshly soul are empty prayers.[3]

Q12. But how does real faith come?

2.3 Romans 10:17 answers the question "But how does real faith come?" And the Romans passage says, "So then faith *cometh* by hearing, and hearing by the word of God."

If we are to have real faith, we must study the Word of God and find out what is promised in it, then believe what the only living God of truth has decreed. Faith must have a guarantee. Trying to believe something that you want to believe is not faith. Believing what God says in His Word is faith. If I am to have faith when I pray, I must find a real promise, an absolute declaration of the LORD in the Word of God on which to rest my faith, trust, and belief.

Furthermore, faith comes through God the Holy Spirit. The Spirit knows the will and Word of God. If I pray in the Spirit and look to the Spirit to teach me God's will, He will lead me out in prayer along the line of God's Word and give me faith that the prayer is to be answered. In no case does real faith come by simply determining that you are going to get the thing that you want to get. Trying to force oneself to believe, either intellectually or emotionally, is not faith but is merely someone operating out of their own fleshliness.

3. To the Christian: "But let him ask in faith, nothing wavering" (James 1:6, KJV). If we are to have faith when we pray, we must know God's Word on which our faith must rest. Following is a list of decrees from God's Word. (The words in *italics* were added for flow)

    3.1 Unconditional decree: "For by grace are ye saved through faith; and that not of yourselves: *it is* the gift of God: Not of works, lest any man should boast…*for* These things have I written unto you that believe on the name of the Son of God; that ye may know that ye have eternal life...*and by the* holy Spirit of God, whereby ye are sealed unto the day of redemption.[4]"

3.2 Conditional decree: God will listen. "Now we know that God heareth not sinners: but if any man be a worshipper of God, and doeth his will, him He heareth...And this is the confidence that we have in him, that, if we ask any thing according to his will, he heareth us...*Thus* if ye abide in me, and my words abide in you, ye shall ask what ye will, and it shall be done unto you."[5]

3.3 Conditional decree:God will protect. "And call upon me in the day of trouble: I will deliver thee, and thou shalt glorify me... *For he* is a buckler to them that walk uprightly... For thou, LORD, wilt bless the righteous; with favour wilt thou compass him as *with* a shield."[6]

3.4 Conditional decree: God will give wisdom. "The fear of the LORD is the beginning of wisdom: a good understanding have all they that do *his commandments*...If any of you lack wisdom," says James, "let him ask of God, that giveth to all *men* liberally, and upbraideth not; and it shall be given him. But let him ask in faith, nothing wavering.

For he that wavereth is like a wave of the sea driven with the wind and tossed."[7]

3.5 Conditional decree: God will bless. "And ye shall serve the LORD your God, and he shall bless thy bread, and thy water; and I will take sickness away from the midst of thee…Return, ye backsliding children, *and* I will heal your backslidings… *For* the LORD will give grace and glory: no good thing will he withhold from them that walk uprightly."[8]

3.6 Unconditional decree: "Then shall he say, Depart from me, ye cursed, into everlasting fire, prepared for the devil and his angels…And these shall go away into everlasting punishment…And whosoever was not found written in the book of life was cast into the lake of fire."[9]

The decrees of the LORD are those statements in the Bible in which it is avowed that God shall do something, and when the Bible says the LORD shall do something, one can take it as a guaranty, a promise that it will be done. Also, there are two kinds of decrees in the Word of the LORD. There are unconditional and conditional decrees, and all the decrees of the LORD will be done as God has arranged to do them.

Q13. How many Christians pray using the promises or decrees of God, assuming that they are *all* unconditional and, based on this false assumption, receive no answer to their prayers?

4

> O, how unreasonable is mankind and how easily the desires of the flesh deceive! If you neglected to water a fig tree, you would not wonder for a moment why it bore no fruit. Then, when you are neglecting to water the soul in vigorous, spiritual nourishment, why do you wonder at your being so spiritually fruitless?[1]

1. In a parable in the Gospel of Luke, Jesus teaches with great emphasis the lesson that Christians should regularly pray and not give up. The parable is found in Luke 18:1–8, which instructs, "And he spake a parable unto them *to this end*, that men always ought to pray, and not to faint" (KJV).

   In other words, God delights in the holy boldness of regular, persistent prayer. It is an expression of great faith, and nothing pleases God the Father, God the Son, and God the Holy Spirit more than the exercise of faith.

   Yet, the LORD does not always let us get things at our first attempt. He would train us and make us strong prayer warriors by compelling us to work hard for the best things. So also, He does not always give us what we ask in answer to the first prayer; He would train us and make us stronger soldiers in His army by compelling us to pray hard for the best things.

1.1 Some would have us believe that it shows unbelief to pray twice for the same thing, that we ought to "take it" the first time that we ask. Doubtless, there are times when we are able through faith in the Word or the lead of the Holy Spirit to claim what we have asked of God at the first supplication; but beyond question, there are other times when we must pray again and again and again for the same thing before we get our answer.

2. "If ye abide in me, and my words abide in you, ye shall ask what ye will, and it shall be done unto you" (John 15:7, KJV). The beauty of prayer is found in these words of our LORD and Savior. Here is prayer that has unbounded power: "Ask what ye will, and it shall be done unto you" (KJV)

2.1 There is a way then of asking and getting precisely what we ask and getting all we ask. Yes, but Christ gives two foundational parts of this all-prevailing prayer:

2.1.1 The first part is "If ye abide in me." What is it to abide in Christ? In John 15, The LORD Jesus Christ had been comparing Himself to a vine and His disciples to the branches in the vine. Some branches were in the vine, that is, were in living union with the vine, so that the sap or life of the vine constantly flowed into these branches. They had no independent life of their own. Everything in them was simply the outcome of the life of the vine flowing into them. Their buds, their leaves, their blossoms, their fruit were really not theirs, but the buds, leaves, blossoms, and fruit of the vine.

To abide in Christ, one must of course already be in Christ through the receiving of Christ as an atoning Savior from the guilt of sin, a risen Savior from the power of sin, as Christ the LORD and Master over all thy life.

Thus being in Christ means our desires will not be our own desires, but Christ's, and our prayers will not in reality be our own prayers but

Christ praying in us. Such prayers will always be in harmony with God's will and Word, and the Father heareth Him always. When our prayers fail, it is because they are indeed our prayers. We have conceived the desire and framed the petition of our self, instead of looking to the LORD Jesus Christ to pray through us.

Q14. How does one reach the spiritual place of abiding in Christ, abiding to the spiritual point that we have no selfish will but only Christ's will? Answer: absolute surrender to God (See appendix A for "Absolute surrender")

2.1.2 But there is a second part stated in John 15:7: "And my words abide in you."

If we are to obtain from God all that we ask from Him, then God's Word must abide and continue in us. We must study His Word, fairly devour His Word, let it sink into our thoughts and into our soul, keep it in our memory, constantly obey it in our life, and let His Word shape and mold our daily life and our every thought and act.

This is the way of abiding in Christ. It is through the Word of God that Jesus imparts Himself to us. The words He speaks unto us, they are spirit and they are life (John 6:63, KJV). It is vain to expect power in prayer unless we meditate much upon the Word of the LORD and let it sink deep and find a permanent abode in our soul. There are many who wonder why they are so powerless in prayer, but the very simple explanation of it all is found in their regular neglect of God's Word.

Think of the Psalmist, his love for God's Word and how often the LORD graced him with heavenly blessings above temporal blessings[2]. Let us desire the Word of the LORD as the Psalmist longed for it. Let us call out to the only living God of the universe and ask the Almighty to cultivate the love of His Word in our soul. Consider the words of the Psalmist as he sings about God's Holy-inspired Word and praise God with him:

> "Thy word have I hid in mine heart, that I might not sin against thee…I will meditate in thy precepts, and have respect unto thy ways…I shall observe it with [my] whole heart…This [is] my comfort in my affliction: for thy word hath quickened me…O how love I thy law! it [is] my meditation all the day…Order my steps in thy word: and let not any iniquity have dominion over me…Make thy face to shine upon thy servant; and teach me thy statutes…Thy word [is] very pure: therefore thy servant loveth it…Thy word [is] true [from] the beginning: and every one of thy righteous judgments [endureth] for ever…*and* I rejoice at thy word."[3]

It is not by moments of rapturous emotional experiences that we learn to abide in Christ; it is by feeding upon God's Holy-inspired Word and looking to God the Holy Spirit to implant these words in our soul and to make them a living, active, rejoiceful thing in our life.

If the Bible thus abides in us, God's Word will stir us up in prayer. It will be the mold in which our prayers are shaped, and our prayers will be necessarily along the line of God's will and will prevail with Him. Prevailing prayer is almost an impossibility where there is neglect of the accurate study of the covenantal Word of God.

Q15. If we know more about church traditions, politics, television shows, fishing, movie stars, and sports teams than we do God's Word, then what will be the result of our prayer life and ultimately our day-to-day life?

5

It is necessary to repeat again and again that prayer, as a mere habit, as a performance gone through by routine or as a job, is a dead and rotten thing. Such mumbling has no connection with the praying for which we plead. We are stressing true praying, which engages and sets on fire every high element of the Christian's being which is born of vital oneness with Christ and the fullness of the Holy Spirit, which springs from the deep, overflowing fountains of tender compassion, deathless concern for man's eternal good; a consuming zeal for the glory of God, and of the imperative need of God's mightiest help. Praying grounded on these solemn and profound convictions is powerful praying.[1]

1. There are two words often overlooked in the lesson about prayer that Paul gives us in Philippians 4:6, 7: "Be careful for nothing; but in every thing by prayer and supplication with thanksgiving let your requests be made known unto God. And the peace of God, which passeth all understanding, shall keep your hearts and

minds through Christ Jesus" (KJV). The two important words often overlooked are "with thanksgiving."

1.1 One reason so many of our prayers lack power is we have neglected to return thanks for blessings already received. God is deeply grieved by the thanklessness and ingratitude of which so many of us are guilty. When Jesus healed the ten lepers and only one came back to give Him thanks, He exclaimed in wonderment and pain, "…Were there not ten cleansed? but where *are* the nine?" (Luke 17:17, KJV).

Thanksgiving to God is one of the inevitable results of being filled with God the Holy Spirit, and one who does not learn "to give thanks in everything" cannot continue to pray in the Spirit. If we would learn to pray with power, we would do well to let these two words sink deep, deep into our soul and life: "with thanksgiving." For thus says the Word of the LORD, "In every thing give thanks: for this is the will of God in Christ Jesus concerning you" (1Thessalonians 5:18, KJV).

Q16. Many thank God, and that is good, but when is the last time we told God why we were thankful. Thus, what are you thankful to God for, and why are you thankful to God for it?

Thanks should always follow answered prayer. No matter what the answer was, we should always be thankful to the LORD. For just as the mist of earth's gratitude rises when the sun of heaven's love warms the ground, so should our thanksgivings rise to the LORD. Has the LORD been gracious to you, and inclined his ear to the voice of your supplication? Then thank him as long as you live. Let the ripe fruit of thanksgiving drop upon the fertile soil from which it drew its life.

To forget to thank God is to refuse to benefit ourselves; for thanksgiving, like prayer, is one great means of promoting the growth of the spiritual life. It helps to remove our burdens, to excite our hope, to increase our faith. It is a healthful and invigorating exercise which quickens the pulse of the believer, and strengthens one for fresh enterprises in his Master's service[2].

2. A hindrance to prayer is found in James 4:3. "Ye ask, and receive not, because ye ask amiss, that ye may consume *it* upon your lusts" (KJV).

A selfish purpose in prayer robs prayer of power. A lot of prayers are selfish. These may be prayers for things which are perfectly proper to ask, for things which it is the will of God to give, but the motive of the prayer is entirely wrong, and so the prayer falls powerless to the ground.

One should be governed by love for the LORD without selfish views, resolving to make the unconditional love of God the end of all one's actions. Without self-centeredness, one could even take up a straw from the ground for the love of God, seeking Him only and nothing else, not even for God's rewards.[3] For thus saith the Word of the LORD:

> Whether therefore ye eat, or drink, or whatsoever ye do, do all to the glory of God. First Corinthians 10:31 (KJV)

Q17. The true purpose in prayer is that God may be glorified in the answer. Thus, let us think of our prayers and ask, "How will the answer we want bring glory to the LORD of hosts in the way He wants to be glorified?"

2.1 Many pray for a revival. That certainly is a prayer that is pleasing to God. It is along the line of His will; but many prayers for revivals are purely selfish. Some churches desire revivals in order that the membership may be increased. For such low purposes, churches and ministers are oftentimes praying for a revival, and oftentimes too, God does not answer the prayer.

So why should we pray for a revival? For the glory of God! So those who are damned to hell will be quickened by God (Ephesians 2:1–10, KJV), and as the saved, they will glorify God. So the babes in Christ will grow in the Spirit and thereby, glorify God more and more. So the mature in Christ will keep growing deeper in Christ and thereby, glorify God more and more and more. To glorify God means we do what God wants the way God wants things done, and the Bible tells us everything God wants and the way He wants it done.

3. Another hindrance to prayer we find in Isaiah 59:1–2: "Behold, the LORD's hand is not shortened, that it cannot save; neither his ear heavy, that it cannot hear: But your iniquities have separated between you and your God, and your sins have hid *his* face from you, that he will not hear" (KJV).

3.1 Sin hinders prayer. Many a person prays and prays and prays and gets absolutely no answer. They do not receive a "yes" or "no" or even a "wait." They receive nothing. Perhaps they are tempted to think that it is not the will of God to answer, or they may think that the days when God answered prayer, if He ever did, are over.

"'Not so,' said Isaiah, 'God's ear is just as open to hear as ever, His hand just as mighty to save. But there is a hindrance. That hindrance is one's own open, shameless, unrepentant sins. Your iniquities have separated between you and your God, and your sins have hid His face from you that He will not hear you.'" (Isaiah 59:1–2, KJV).

3.2 Anyone who would have power in prayer must be merciless in dealing with one's own unrepentant sins. For thus saith God's Word, "If I regard iniquity in my heart, the LORD will not hear *me*" (Psalms 66:18, KJV).

Here are some ways to identify spiritual problem areas that can hinder or stifle prayer. Biblically, start with the battleground of the world and flesh. According to passages such as Galatians 5:19–21; Proverbs 6:16–19; Mark 7:21–23; Colossians 3:8; Exodus 20; James 4:4–5; Luke 13:5; 1Corinthians 6:9–10; Leviticus 18:22–23, 20:13; Romans 1:26–27; 1 John 4:20, look for any habitual problem areas of repeated, willful unrepentant sinning:

- adultery/fornication (mind, body and/or emotions)

- putting anything before the LORD
- witchcraft, sorcery, necromancy, fortune telling
- unrighteous anger/murders/hatred
- not keeping the LORD's day
- strife/divisions/factions (purposeful discord)
- heresies (teachings that contradict foundational biblical truths)
- envyings/covetousness
- drunkenness/greed/gluttony
- revellings (riotous behavior)
- evil thoughts/wicked imaginings
- fornication, homosexuality, incest, bestiality
- making and/or worshiping a graven image[4]
- thefts/extortion (taking what does not belong to you)
- lying (purposeful falsehood)
- taking God's name and/or titles in vain/blasphemy/vilifying the Trinity
- pride (self-importance)
- foolishness/Filthy communication (vulgarity)
- not honoring thy father and mother

- friendship with the world (syncretism and/or compromise of the faith)
- slander/backbiting/rumor-mongering/murmuring (complaining)

Unrepentant sins stifle our prayer life! Yes, Christians will sin, but we were not born again to live a life of unrepentant sinning. Sadly, many Christians of the world today have no idea how stifling their unrepentant sin is to their prayer life and biblically have next-to-no idea what to do about their unrepentant sins. Following is what Christians are to do biblically with unrepentant sin in their life:

First, confess the sin that has gotten a foothold in your life, and ask God to forgive you in the name of Jesus. For thus says the word of the LORD, "If we confess our sins, he is faithful and just to forgive us *our* sins, and to cleanse us from all unrighteousness" (1 John 1:9, KJV).

Secondly, actively repent of the sin. That is, stop doing the sin and ask the LORD to replace it with obedience in following after the LORD Jesus Christ. For thus saith the Word of the LORD, "Bring forth therefore fruits meet for repentance" (Matthew 3:8, KJV). Remember, true salvation does not lead to a life of unrepentant sinning (Matthew 7:17, KJV).

Q18. Why is it that some people, even some churchgoers, seem to believe that there is no consequence to unconfessed/ unrepentant sinning? (Consider Luke 13:5; Psalms 66:18; 1Corinthians 5:6–7; Revelation 3:14–19, KJV).

4. Still another hindrance to prayer is found in Ezekiel 14:3: "These men have set up their idols in their heart, and put the stumbling block of their iniquity before their face: should I be enquired of at all by them" (KJV)?

4.1 What is an idol put up in the heart? Here in Ezekiel, we have a clear violation of the first commandment. The first commandment basically teaches that nothing and nobody is to come before the LORD in importance. God alone has the right to the supreme place in our soul. Everything and everyone else must be secondary to the blessed Trinity.

Q19. What are some things of the world and/or church that are as "an idol put up in the heart?"

> "Set your affection on things above, not on things on the earth."[5] Unless we live by the Bible, we cannot be spiritual. A little affection for the things of earth robs the soul of spiritual life. In this matter, Beelzebub is an excellent reasoner. He will suggest that your desires are only for the glory of God, that you have no affection for the worldly object but desire it only for God's glory.[6]

4.2 We need to be wary how we desire earthly things for God's glory. Many good deeds, church traditions, religious paraphernalia, and so-called ministries seem to more closely resemble idolatry than glorify God. For example, the Pharisees turned their traditions into things that were more important than God. For thus declarith the Bible:

> And he said unto them, Full well ye reject the commandment of God, that ye may keep your own tradition…*and* Beware lest any man spoil you through philosophy and vain deceit, after the tradition of men, after the rudiments of the world, and not after Christ.
>
> Mark 7:9–13, Colossians 2:8 (KJV)

6

By prayer the windows of heaven are opened, and showers of refreshing dew are rained upon the soul. It is as a watered garden, a fertile spot where blooms the unfading rose of Sharon and the lily-of-the-valley;[1] where spread the undecaying, unwithering branches of the tree of life.

By prayer the soul is nourished and strengthened by the divine life. Do you long for a brighter hope and deeper joy, for a deeper sense of the divine fullness, for a sweeter, closer walk with the only living God, the LORD? Then live in prayer. Do you love to feel the holy flame of love burning in all its intensity in your soul? Then enkindle it often at the golden altar of prayer. Without prayer, the soul will weaken, famish, and sicken; the fountain of love dry up and become as a thirsty and parched desert.[2]

1. The great need of the day is a Holy Spirit revival. But let us consider first of all what a Holy Spirit revival is.

1.1 As we understand from John 6:63, revival is a time of quickening or impartation of life. As God alone can give life, a revival is a time when God visits His people and by the power of God the Holy Spirit imparts new life to them. Through them he imparts life to sinners dead in trespasses and sins.

A manmade revival is not the same as a Holy Spirit revival. A manmade revival is organized, constructed and delivered by man. It may even be done in God's name but has man's goals in mind. Ultimately, the difference between man's revival and God's revival is that God starts and empowers a Holy Spirit-filled revival. He is its focus, and He determines its outcome. God's revival will use man, but has God as the focus from beginning to end.

Q20. Do we want a true Holy Spirit revival, a revival that will bring change— change to the lost and the saved and change to the church locally and at large? Are we willing to pray, "Holy Spirit come and bring a revival, no matter the cost, no matter the change?"

2. Look at the present spiritual condition of the church and ask, "Is it any wonder that the lost are no longer flocking to the church?"

   2.1 Look at the present state of the church. We have church member after church member who keep this tradition and that tradition but cannot explain *why* they do what they do or why they believe in what they say they believe in. How is a lack of spiritual understanding a good evangelism tool? It is not and never will be. For thus saith the Word of the LORD:

   > My people are destroyed for lack of knowledge.
   >
   > Hosea 4:6 (KJV) The Hebrew word here used for destroy means suffer.

   2.2 Worldliness is just as rampant among church members as among the lost of the world. Many church members are just as eager as any in the rush to get rich. They use the methods of the world in the accumulation of wealth, and they hold just as fast to it as any when they get it. Furthermore then, they bring their get-rich-quick schemes and business practices into the church. All in the name of helping the church, they then reduce evangelism to marketing Jesus like a toothbrush.

2.3 Prayerlessness abounds among church members on every hand. Some one has said that Christians on the average do not spend more than five minutes a day in prayer. Neglect of the Word of God goes hand in hand with neglect of prayer to the LORD. Very many Christians spend twice as much time every day wallowing through the sewage of the daily papers as they do bathing in the cleansing laver of God's Holy Word.

Q21. Oh children of God how much time do we spend:

____: On the computer
____: Playing games or exercising
____: Watching television or movies
____: Going from worldly activity to worldly activity
____: Eating food
____: Going to the bathroom
____: Reading the Bible
____: Talking at God and not listening
____: Serious one-on-one time communicating with God. No distractions, no multi-tasking while praying, just you

and God one-on-one like in Matthew 6:6.

2.4 Along with neglect of prayer and neglect of the Word of God goes the neglect for the LORD's Day. It is fast becoming a day of worldly pleasure instead of a day of holy rest and service. The television, together with its inane twaddle and filthy scandal, takes the place of the Bible; and yard work, and golf, and bicycling, the place of the Sunday school and church service.

Q22. There are many good intending, well-meaning people out there who love the LORD with all their heart and diligently serve Him with their mustard seed of faith. But what about all the rest who call themselves Christians?

After regular shameless, unrepentant neglect of God's Word, shunning prayer, and willfully disregarding God's Ten Commandments, do people who call themselves Christians find themselves in the lost church referred to in Revelation 3:16–19 that, by the decree of God and not man, is damned to hell if it never repents? For consider what the Word of God says:

> He that hath an ear, let him hear what the Spirit saith unto the churches… I know thy works, that thou art neither cold nor hot: I would thou wert cold or hot. So then because thou art lukewarm, and neither cold nor hot, I will spue thee out of my mouth…As many as I love, I rebuke and chasten: be zealous therefore, and repent.
>
> Revelation 3:13, 15–16, 19 (KJV)

3. Sons and daughters of the only living God, we need a revival—deep, widespread, general—in the power of God the Holy Spirit. It is either a general revival or the dissolution of the church, of the family, and of the country. A revival, new life from God, is the cure, and the only cure that will stem the awful tide of immorality, unbelief and our nation collapsing into 666 (Revelation 13, KJV).

   The great need of today is a general revival. The need is clear. It admits of no honest difference of opinion. What then shall we do? Pray. Take up the Psalmist's prayer, "Revive us again, that Thy people may rejoice in Thee."[3] Take up Ezekiel's prayer to God to "Come from the four winds, O breath, and breathe upon these slain, that they may live.[4] Hark, I hear a noise! Behold a shaking! I can almost feel the breeze upon my cheek. I can almost see the great living army rising to their feet. Shall we not pray and pray and pray and pray, till the Spirit comes, and God revives His people again?

Q23. Will the children of God pray for a revival, that is, a true Holy Spirit revival? Will we pray for a revival no matter the cost, no matter the change? Will you pray?

Yes:_______ No:_______

APPENDIX A

Absolute Surrender[1]

Our God in heaven answers the prayers which you have offered for blessing on yourselves and for blessing on others by this one demand: *Are you willing to surrender yourselves absolutely into His hands*? What is your answer to be?

Yes:_____ No: _____

1. Let me say to the children of God, first of all, that God claims it from us.

A. God Expects Your Surrender

God expects our surrender, but who is God to expect such a thing? Who is God? He is the only living LORD of Hosts, the Almighty Trinity, the Fountain of life, the only Source of existence and power and goodness. Throughout the universe, there is nothing good but what God works. God has created the sun, the moon, the stars, the flowers, the trees, and the grass. Are they not all absolutely surrendered to Him who made them?

The LORD is their Creator and does not He work in them just what He pleases? When God clothes the lily with its beauty, is it not yielded up, surrendered, given over to God as He works in it and with it? And God's redeemed children, oh, can you think that the Almighty will do His work if there is only half or a part of them surrendered?

Think of how irrational and unbiblical it would sound for God to work with a half or a part of a believer: "God, you can use my mind, but not my soul." or "God you can use my body, but not my emotions." When God comes to claim our surrender, the surrender is all-encompassing and total.

B. Surrender

You know in daily life what absolute surrender is. You know that everything has to be given up to its special, definite object and service (Romans 9:21–23, KJV). I have a pen in my pocket, and that pen is absolutely surrendered to the one work of writing. That pen must be absolutely surrendered to my hand if I am to write. Now, do you expect that in your immortal being, in the divine nature that you have received by regeneration, God will work His work, every day and every hour, unless you are entirely given up to Him, entirely surrendered to Him?

The temple of Solomon was absolutely surrendered to God; it was not half used for pagan worship and half used for worshiping the LORD. And every one of us is a temple of God in which God the Holy Spirit will dwell and work mightily on one condition-absolute surrender to Him. God claims it; God is worthy of it, and without it God shall not work His blessed work in us.

2. The Almighty not only claims it, but God will work it Himself.

A. God Accomplishes Your Surrender

I come with a message to those who are fearful and anxious. God does not ask you to give the perfect surrender in your strength, or by the power of your will; the LORD is willing to work it in you. Do we not read: "it is God that worketh in you both to will and to do of *his* good pleasure" (Philippians 2:13, KJV)? And that is what we should seek, to go on our faces before our Creator, until our soul knows that the everlasting God Himself will come in to turn out what is wrong. He will conquer what is evil and work what is well pleasing in His blessed sight. God Himself will work it in you.

Q24. Are you willing to pray, "LORD God Almighty please surrender me! Work

> Philippians 2:13 upon my soul, emotions, mind, body and life. Bring me O LORD under the totality of your will, so that thy will is my will."

B. Fear Not

I want to encourage you, and I want you to cast away every fear. Come with that feeble desire and pray. If there is the fear which says, "Oh, my desire is not strong enough. I am not willing for everything that may come, and I do not feel bold enough to say I can conquer everything." I implore you, learn to know and trust our God now. Say: "My God, I am willing that You should surrender me."

If there is anything holding you back or any sacrifice you are afraid of making, come to the LORD of Hosts now and prove how gracious our God is. Do not be afraid that He will command from you what He will not bestow upon you. Come and trust God to work in you that absolute surrender to Himself.

APPENDIX B

Don't pray in the name of Jehovah, because that is not God's name.

Now, has anyone out there ever heard God referred to as *Jehovah*? Maybe one has heard the word *Jehovah* in a song or a Bible study, but chances are if you have been in church for any length of time you have heard God called Jehovah.

If you have a King James Bible, you can find *Jehovah* used in Exodus 6:3, Psalms 83:18, Isaiah 12:2, and Isaiah 26:4. However, unless the Old Testament was written in King James English, then we have a few biblical difficulties with God's name being *Jehovah*. What?

The original Hebrew language did not use vowels, thus as you look at *Jehovah*, one needs to ask, "Where did they get the vowels from?" Also, the word *Jehovah* is never used in the original Bible manuscripts of Hebrew or Aramaic.

Stop, and think about it for a moment: if the Hebrew language did not use vowels, and *Jehovah* obviously uses vowels, and if *Jehovah* is in none of the original Hebrew or Aramaic text of the Bible, then where did we get the word *Jehovah*, and why do we assume it's God's name?

The problem does not originate with the Bible in its original writings. No, the Bible is holy inspired and true in all its parts (2 Timothy 3:16, KJV). The difficulty occurred in the translation of the Bible from ancient Hebrew into the languages of English and German. So what happened?

When Moses was on the mountain with the LORD and asked, "Whom should I say sent me?" God's response was basically "I AM" (Exodus 3:14, KJV). The Hebrew during Moses's day used only consonants, thus God's name *I AM* would have been spelled *YHWH*.

Furthermore, it was not until several hundred years later after the Babylonian captivity that the Hebrews started using vowels. In those Old Testament days, the Jews believed saying God's holy name *YHWH* would break the third Commandment (Exodus 20:7, KJV).

To insure that no one would say "YHWH," they used the word *Adonai* and put the vowels from *Adonai* all around the name *YHWH*. Thus, when someone was reading the scriptures aloud, instead of saying "YHWH," they would know to say "Adonai." Following is a very simple example of this principle: *Y a H o W a H e*.

Sadly, the early Bible translators were not aware of this rule, and when they saw the Hebrew consonants *Y*, *H*, *W*, and *H* surrounded by the vowels *a*, *o*, *a*, and *e*, together they thought they had the whole name of God as *Jehovah*.

However, by no stretch of biblical Hebrew or Aramaic is *Jehovah* God's name. It is not a construct of God's name, and it is not a derivative of God's name. No, *Jehovah* is simply a conjunction of two different word's vowels and consonants.

In biblical Hebrew, all the names and titles of God specifically tell us something about the LORD, such as that He is our Creator, our Redeemer, etc. The word "Jehovah" tells us nothing about the God of the Bible since it is not His name.

So is there anything wrong with calling God "Jehovah"? It is not blasphemy to call God by the word *Jehovah*, but it is not respectful either. *Jehovah* is not God's name, so don't call or pray to the Almighty by what He is not.

BIBLIOGRAPHY

Bounds, Edward M. *Power Through Prayer*. http://www.ccel.org/ccel/bounds/power.txt.

Griffin, Justin. *The Truth about Images of Jesus and the Second Commandment*. Mustang, OK: Tate Publishing. 2006.

Lawrence, Brother. *The Practice of the Presence of God*. London: The Epworth Press. http://www.ccel.org/ccel/lawrence/practice.i.html.

Murray, Andrew. *Absolute Surrender*. Chicago: Moody Press. 1895. http://www.ccel.org/ccel/murray/surrender.txt.

Orr, James. *How to Live a Holy Life*. http://www.ccel.org/ccel/orr/holylife.txt.

Spurgeon, Charles Haddon. *Morning and Evening: Daily Readings*. http://www.ccel.org/ccel/spurgeon/morneve.txt.

Torrey, Reuben Archer. *How to Pray*. http://www.ccel.org/ccel/torrey/pray.txt.

NOTES

Introduction

1. Adapted from *The Truth About Images of Jesus and the Second Commandment*, (Mustang, OK: Tate Publishing) 2006, 12.

Chapter 1

1. Adapted from *Practice of the Presence of God*, Third Conversation. http://www.ccel.org/ccel/lawrence/practice.iii.iii.html
2. Mark 12:29–30 (KJV); Deuteronomy 6:6 (KJV); 2 Corinthians 3:3(KJV)
3. 1 John 5:7 (KJV).

Chapter 2

1. Adapted from *How To Live a Holy Life*, Section on Prayer. http://www.ccel.org/ccel/orr/holylife.txt.

2. Hebrews 10:19 (KJV) Having therefore, brethren, boldness to enter into the holiest by the blood of Jesus,

Chapter 3

1. Adapted from *How to Live a Holy Life,* Section on Prayer. http://www.ccel.org/ccel/orr/holylife.txt.
2. Adapted from *Morning and Evening Readings*, October 8—Evening Reading. http://www.ccel.org/ccel/spurgeon/morneve.txt.
3. Adapted from *Morning and Evening Readings*, January 2—Morning Reading. http://www.ccel.org/ccel/spurgeon/morneve.txt.
4. Ephesians 2:8–9; 1John 5:13; Romans 10:9; John 3:16. Salvation is free. Receiving the LORD Jesus Christ is a gift given by God. Romans 6:23; Romans 5:11 ; Ephesians 3:5 and Ephesians 4:30.
5. John 9:31; Psalm 10:17; 1John 5:14; John 15:7.
6. Psalms 50:15; Proverbs 2:7; Psalms 5:12; Deuteronomy 31:6; Psalms 91:14–15; 1 Corinthians 10:13.
7. Psalms 111:10; John 14:26; Luke 21:15; Psalms 18:28; James 1:5–6.
8. Exodus 23:25; Jeremiah 3:22; Psalms 84:11; Philippians 4:19; Romans 15:13.

9. Luke 13:5; Matthew 25:31–46; Revelation 20:15.

Chapter 4

1. Adapted from *How to Live a Holy Life*, Section on Spiritual Dryness. http://www.ccel.org/ccel/orr/holylife.txt.
2. Temporal blessings are those earthly good things that for a season fall upon the just and the unjust alike. Matthew 5:45 says, "… for he maketh his sun to rise on the evil and on the good, and sendeth rain on the just and on the unjust".
3. Psalms 119:11, 15, 34, 50, 97, 133, 135, 140, 160, 162.

Chapter 5

1. Adapted from *Power through Prayer*, Chapter 5. http://www.ccel.org/ccel/bounds/power.txt.
2. Adapted from *Morning and Evening Readings*, October 30—Morning Reading. http://www.ccel.org/ccel/spurgeon/morneve.txt.
3. Adapted from *Practice of the Presence of God*, Second Conversation. http://www.ccel.org/ccel/lawrence/practice.iii.ii.html
4. For a deeper understanding of this sin and how much the LORD hates this sin see the book,

"The Truth about Images of Jesus and the Second Commandment" by Rev Justin Griffin.

5. Colossians 3:2
6. Adapted from *How To Live a Holy Life*, Section on Spiritual Dryness. http://www.ccel.org/ccel/orr/holylife.txt.

Chapter 6

1. Song of Solomon 2:1 "I am the rose of Sharon, and the lily of the valleys."
2. Adapted from *How To Live a Holy Life*, Section on Prayer. http://www.ccel.org/ccel/orr/holylife.txt.
3. Psalms 85:6 "Wilt thou not revive us again: that thy people may rejoice in thee?"
4. Ezekiel 37:9 "Then said he unto me, Prophesy unto the wind, prophesy, son of man, and say to the wind, Thus saith the LORD GOD; Come from the four winds, O breath, and breathe upon these slain, that they may live."

Appendix A

1. Adapted from *Absolute Surrender*, Chapter 1. http://www.ccel.org/ccel/murray/surrender.txt.